Robert Underwood Johnson

**Songs of Liberty and Other Poems**

Robert Underwood Johnson

**Songs of Liberty and Other Poems**

ISBN/EAN: 9783744770163

Printed in Europe, USA, Canada, Australia, Japan

Cover: Foto ©Andreas Hilbeck / pixelio.de

More available books at **www.hansebooks.com**

# SONGS OF LIBERTY AND OTHER POEMS

BY

ROBERT UNDERWOOD JOHNSON

INCLUDING PARAPHRASES FROM THE SERVIAN
AFTER TRANSLATIONS BY NIKOLA TESLA, WITH A
PREFATORY NOTE BY HIM ON SERVIAN POETRY

NEW YORK
THE CENTURY CO.
1897

TO MAURICE FRANCIS EGAN

# CONTENTS

# SONGS OF LIBERTY AND OTHER POEMS

# APOSTROPHE TO GREECE *

## FROM THE PARTHENON

INSCRIBED TO THE GREEK PEOPLE ON THE SEVENTY-
FIFTH ANNIVERSARY OF THEIR INDEPENDENCE)

### I

O LAND of sage and stoic—
Of human deeds heroic,
  Of heroes' deeds divine!
What braggart of the nations
Shall scorn thy proud narrations—
Thou who hast named the stars from thy Olympian line!

* This ode, begun on the steps of the Parthenon in 1886, was
published in the New York " Independent " of April, 1896, and, in
part, in modern Greek in the " Hellas," a record of the Olympic
Games of that year.

I

In spite of Moslem crime
Thou livest!   Hungry Time
   Can only dead devour.
Though asphodel hath strewed
This marble solitude,
The silence thrills with life, the ruins rise in power.

Yon sea's imperial vastness
Was once thy friend and fastness;
   By many a curving strand,
'Twixt purple capes, on edges
Of seaward-looking ledges,
Rose the white cities sown by thy adventurous hand.

Nor couldst thou think of these
As lonely colonies
   Wherewith rich Corinth lined
The West, while Dorian sails
Outrode Ægean gales;
Nay, suburbs were they all, molds of Athenian mind.

Then could thy galleys pass
From Tyre to Acragas,
   By Grecian islands gray
That dreamed of Athens' brow,
And gaily to the prow
Harnessed the pawing winds to seek some Attic bay.

Here to Athene's feast,
From West, from North, from East—
   Through Jason's fabled strait
Or round Malea's rock—
The homesick sails would flock,
with an Odyssey of peril to relate.

And what exultant stir
When the swart islander,
   Bound for the festal week,
First saw Colonna's crest
Give back the glowing West
past Ægina's shore and her prophetic peak!

I hear his cheery cries
Though Time between us lies
   More wide than sea and land.
The gladness that he brings
Thrills in the song he sings,
ching his welcome craft on Phaleron's level strand.

O harbor of delight!
Strike the torn sail—to-night
   On Attic soil again!
When joy is free to slaves
What though the swarming waves
ow each other down like the generations of men!

Now, for a time, to war
And private hate a bar
    Of sacred armistice;
Even in the under-world
Shall the rough winds be furled
That tell of wrangling shades that crowd the courts of D

'T is Peace shall bring the green
For Merit's brow. What scene,
    O Athens, shall be thine!
Till from Parnassus' height
Phœbus' reluctant light
Lingers along Hymettus' fair and lofty line.

With dance and song and game
And oratory's flame
    Shall Hellas beat and swell,
Till, olive-crowned, in pride
The envied victors ride,
Fellows to those whose fame the prancing marbles te

O antique time and style,
Return to us awhile
    Bright as thy happy skies!
Silent the sounds that mar:
Like music heard afar
The harmony endures while all the discord dies.

Not yet the cloister's shade
Fell on a world afraid,
   Morbid, morose—the alloy
Found greater than the gold
Of life.  Like Nature old
ı still didst sing and show the sanity of joy.

That secret to this day
Hath its enduring sway
   O'er all thy childlike kind.
Oh, teach this anxious age
Through thy serener page
· by the happy heart to keep the unclouded mind.

II

But thou wert Freedom's too
As well as Joy's, and drew
   From every mountain breast
An air that could endure
No foreign foe—so pure
Lycabettus neighbors the Corinthian crest.

Nor was thy love of life
For thee alone.  Thy strife
   Was for the race, no less.
Thee, to whom wrong is done
While wrong confronts the sun,
oppressor cannot crush, nor teach thee to oppress.

·

By thee for lands benighted
Was Freedom's beacon lighted
   That now enstars the earth.
Welcome the people's hour!
Passed is the monarch's power,
Dread waits not on his death that trembled at his birtl

As down a craggy steep
Albanian torrents leap
   Impetuous to the sea—
Such was thy ancient spirit,
Still thine.   Who that inherit
Hatred of tyranny inherit not from thee?

Look to the West and see
Thy daughter, Italy—
   Fathered by Neptune bold
On Cumæ's sheltered strand
(Forgot but for the hand
That saved to Art her sibyl many-named and old);

That temple-sated soil,
Whose altar-smoke would coil
   To hide the Avernian steep,
Grows the same harvest now—
Best increase of the plow,
Fair Freedom, of thy seed, sown for the world to reap

Though regal Rome display
The triumphs of her day;
   Though Florence, laurel-hung,
Tell how she held the van
In the slow march of man—
eek was the path they trod, Greek was the song they sung.

Look farther west and there
Behold thy later heir,
   Child of thy Jove-like mind—
Fair France.   How has she kept
The watch while others slept?
.s Wisdom hastened on while Justice lagged behind?

Like thee, full well she knows
Through what maternal throes
   New forms from olden come;
Her arts, her temples, speak
A glory that is Greek,
d filially her heart turns to the ancestral home.

For her no backward look
Into the bloody book
   Of kings.   Thrice-rescued land!
Her furrowed graves bespeak
A nobler fate: to seek
service of the world again the world's command.

She in whose skies of peace
Arise new auguries
   To strengthen, cheer, and guide—
When nations in a horde
Draw the unhallowed sword,
O Memory, walk, a warning specter, at her side!

Among thy debtor lands,
See, grateful England stands;
   Who at thy ranging feet
Learned how to carry Law
Into the jungle's maw,
And tempers unto Man or cold or desert heat.

All that thou daredst she dares
Till now thy name she bears—
   Mother of Colonies.
What if thy glorious Past
She should restore at last,
And clothe in new renown the dream of Pericles!

If she but lean to thee
Once more thy North shall be
   Uplifted from the dust.
Mother of noble men,
Thy friends of sword and pen,
England, though slow to justice, shall again be just.

And now from our new land
Beyond two seas, a hand!
 Our world, for ages dumb,
Part of thy fable-lore,
Gathers upon its shore
ach dying race as soil for one chief race to come.

 But of our beating heart
Thy pulse how large a part!
 Our wider sky but bounds
Another Grecian dawn.
Lament not what is gone;
entelicus grieves not, for Fame hath healed his wounds.

### III

THEN, Hellas! scorn the sneer
Of kings who will not hear
 Their people's moaning voice,
More deaf than shore to sea!
The world hath need of thee—
he world thou still canst teach to reason and rejoice.

 Yes, need of thee while Art
Of life is but a part—
 Plaything or luxury.
Greek soil perchance may show
Where Art's hid stream doth flow—
o rise, a new Alpheus, near another sea.

Yes, need of thee while Gold
Makes timid traitors bold
 To lay republics low;
Not ignorant nor poor
Spread for their feet the lure—
The kind, the loved, the honored, aim the brutal blow.

Yes, need of thee while Earth
Each day shows Heaven a girth
 Of want and misery;
Wherein there is not found
Beyond thy happy bound
A people brave, sane, temperate, thrifty, chaste, and free.

Then, though by faction's blunder,
And boasts, of mimic thunder,
 Again thou be betrayed,
Vain this, vain every treason;
With thee are Hope and Reason,
Nor Past can be forgot, nor Future long delayed.

Troy was, but Athens is—
The World's and Liberty's,
 Nor ever less shall be!
Though fallen are old fanes
The vestal fire remains
Bright with the light serene of immortality.

## SONG OF THE MODERN GREEKS

LIBERTY, beloved of Hellas,
   Lend us once again thy sword;
Turn thy glorious eyes that tell us
   Thou art still to be adored.

Hail thee, spirit! hover over
   Salamis and Marathon,
Till each corse that called thee lover
   Rise with thee to lead us on.

Slumbered Hellas long in sadness,
   Waiting thee to call her forth;
Hushed the very cradle's gladness
   By the tyrant of the North.

Long she dwelt with buried heroes
   In the fame of other years;
But against a horde of Neros
   What availed or pride or tears?

Then at last thy summons called us,
 And as one we followed thee,
Till the rusted chains that thralled us
 Fell, and Greece once more was free.

Ah, but while our kin are weeping
 Over sea and over land,
Let us not again be sleeping,
 Wake us with thy warning hand.

Though the Moslem swarm to slay us,
 Though false friends, within, without—
Kings or cowards—shall betray us,
 If thou lead us, who shall doubt?

Greece's blood made many an altar
 For the nations then unborn;
Will they with her peril palter—
 Give her gratitude, or scorn?

Oh, could Earth and Time assemble
 All thy legions, Liberty,
At their tread the world would tremble
 With the passion to be free.

## TO THE HOUSATONIC AT STOCKBRIDGE

CONTENTED river! in thy peaceful realm—
The cloudy willow and the plumy elm:
They call thee English, thinking thus to mate
Their musing streams that, oft with pause sedate,
Linger through misty meadows for a glance
At haunted tower or turret of romance.
Beware their praise who rashly would deny
To our New World its true tranquillity.
Our " New World "?   Nay, say rather to our Old
(Let truth and freedom make us doubly bold);
Tell them: A thousand silent years before
Their beauteous sea-born isle—at every shore
Dripping like Aphrodite's tresses—rose,
Here, 'neath her purple veil, deep slept Repose,
To be awakened but by wail of war.
From yon soft heights thou com'st; thy heavenly lore,
Like our own childhood's, all the workday toil
Cannot efface, nor long its sweetness soil.
Thou hast grown human laboring with men
At wheel and spindle; sorrow thou dost ken;

Yet dost thou still the unshaken stars behold,
And, calm for calm, return'st them, as of old.
Thus, like a gentle nature that grows strong
In meditation for the strife with wrong,
Thou show'st the peace that only tumult can;
Surely, serener river never ran.

Thou beautiful!  From every dreamy hill
What eye but wanders with thee at thy will,
Imagining thy silver course unseen
Convoyed by two attendant streams of green
In bending lines,—like half-expected swerves
Of swaying music, or those perfect curves
We call the robin; making harmony
With many a new-found treasure of the eye:
With meadows, marging softly rounded hills
Where Nature teemingly the myth fulfils
Of many-breasted Plenty; with the blue,
That to the zenith fades through triple hue,
Pledge of the constant day; with clouds of white,
That haunt horizons with their blooms of light,
And when the east with rosy eve is glowing
Seem like full cheeks of zephyrs gently blowing.

Contented river! and yet over-shy
To mask thy beauty from the eager eye;

Hast thou a thought to hide from field and town?
In some deep current of the sunlit brown
Art thou disquieted—still uncontent
With praise of thy Homeric bard who lent
The world the placidness thou gavest him?
Thee Bryant loved when life was at its brim;
And when the wine was falling, in thy wood
Of sturdy willows like a Druid stood.
Oh, for his touch on this o'er-throbbing time,
His hand upon the hectic brow of Rhyme,
Cooling its fevered passion to a pace
To lead, to stir, to reinspire the race!

.    .    .    .    .    .    .

Ah! there's a restive ripple, and the swift
Red leaves—September's firstlings—faster drift;
Betwixt twin aisles of prayer they seem to pass
One green, one greenly mirrored in thy glass).
Wouldst thou away, dear stream? Come, whisper near!
 also of much resting have a fear:
Let me to-morrow thy companion be
By fall and shallow to the adventurous sea!

## FAREWELL TO ITALY

We lingered at Domo d'Ossola—
    Like a last, reluctant guest—
Where the gray-green tide of Italy
    Flows up to a snowy crest.

The world from that Alpine shoulder
    Yearns toward the Lombard plain—
The hearts that come, with rapture,
    The hearts that go, with pain.

Afar were the frets of Milan;
    Below, the enchanted lakes;
And—*was* it the mist of the evening,
    Or the mist that the memory makes?

We gave to the pale horizon
    The Naples that evening gives;
We reckoned where Rome lies buried,
    And we felt where Florence lives.

And as Hope bends low at parting
    For a death-remembered tone,
We searched the land that Beauty
    And Love have made their own.

We would take of her hair some ringlet,
    Some keepsake from her breast,
And catch of her plaintive music
    The strain that is tenderest.

So we strolled in the yellow gloaming
    (Our speech with musing still)
Till the noise of the militant village
    Fell faint on Calvary Hill.

And scarcely our mood was broken
    Of near-impending loss
To find at the bend of the pathway
    A station of the Cross.

And up through the green aisle climbing
    (Each shrine like a counted bead),
We heard from above the swaying
    And mystical chant of the creed.

Then the dead seemed the only living,
    And the real seemed the wraith,

And we yielded ourselves to the vision
We saw with the eye of Faith.

Then she said, " Let us go no farther :
'T is fit that we make farewell
While forest and lake and mountain
Are under the vesper spell."

As we rested, the leafy silence
Broke like a cloud at play,
And a browned and burdened woman
Passed, singing, down the way.

'T was a song of health and labor, —
Of childlike gladness, blent
With the patience of the toiler
That tyrants call content.

" Nay, this is the word we have waited,"
I said, " that a year and a sea
From now, in our doom of exile,
Shall echo of Italy."

Just then what a burst from the bosquet—
As a bird might have found its soul !
And each by the halt of the heart-throb
Knew 't was the rossignol.

Then we drew to each other nearer
 And drank at the gray wall's verge
The sad, sweet song of lovers,—
 Their passion and their dirge.

And the carol of Toil below us
 And the pæan of Prayer above
Were naught to the song of Sorrow.
 For under the sorrow was Love.

 . . . . . .

Alas ! for the dear remembrance
 We chose for our amulet :
The one that is left to keep it—
 Ah! how can he forget ?

## A CHOPIN FANTASY

ON REMEMBRANCE OF A PRÉLUDE

Come, love, sit here and let us leave awhile
This custom-laden world for warmer lands
Where, 'neath the silken net of afternoon,
Leisure is duty and dread care a dream.

(*The music begins*)

That cliff 's Minorca, that horizon Spain.
There in the west, like fragrance visible,
Rises the soft light as the sun goes down
Till half the sky is palpitant with gold.
Follow it eastward to the gentle blue,
With faith and childhood in it, and the peace
Men agonize and roam for.   See that fleet
That flutters in the breeze from the Camargue
Like white doves, huddled now, now scattering.
(They say all native boats are homeward bound
Against to-morrow's annual festival.)
What peace there is in looking from this height

On palms and olives, and the easy steps
By which the terrace clambers yonder hill!
How dark those hollows whence the roads of white
Ascend in angles to the high-perched town!
Needless the music of the convent bell:
'Tis vespers in the heart as in the air.
This is the hour for love, that, like the breath
Of yonder orange, sweetest is at eve.
Here, safe entwined, what could be wished for two
Hid in an island hidden in the sea?
Now let me lay my head upon your lap,
And place your rose-leaf fingers on my lids,
Lest, catching glimpse of your resplendent eyes,
My ardor should blaspheme the coming stars!

   .    .    .    .    .    .    .    .

How fast it darkens! One must needs be blind
To know the twilight softness of your voice.
And Love,—not blind, but with a curtained sight,—
Like one who dwells with Sorrow, can discern
The shading of a shadow in a tone.
There 's something troubles you, my sweet-of-hearts,
A hesitance in that caressing word;
Nothing unhappy—a presentiment
Such as from far might thrill the under-depths
Of some still tranquil lake before a storm.
Be happy, love, not ponder happiness.

Unerringly I know your woman's soul,
Content to have your happiness put off
Like well-planned feast against to-morrow's need,
And more enjoyed in planning than in use.
But oh, we men, God made us—what was that?
A drop upon your hand?   Perhaps a tear
Lost by an angel who remembers yet
Some perfect moment of th' imperfect world,
And goes reluctantly her way to heaven,
Still envious of our lot?   Another drop!
Why, 't is the rain.   Stand here and see that sky—
Blackness intense as sunlight.   What a chasm
Of silver where that lightning tore its way!
That crash was nearer!   Here 's our shelter—quick!
Now it 's upon us!   Half a breath, and—there!
No wonder you should tremble when the earth
Sways thus and all the firmament 's a-reel.
Tremble, but fear not—Love created Fear
To drive men back to Love, where you are now.
What rhythmic terror in the tideless sea
That wildly seeks the refuge of the rocks
From unknown dangers (dangers known are none)!
God! did you see within the headland's jaws
That drifting sail?   Wait the next flash and—look!
Oh, heaven! to cruise about a hundred coasts,
Safe past the fabled monsters of the deep,

To break supinely on familiar shoals
Where one in childhood digged a mimic grave!

   .    .    .    .    .    .    .    .

Thank God for those few, momentary stars,
And that slow-lifting zone of topaz light,
Like parting guest returning with a smile.
We care not now that the insatiate storm
Plunges with leaps of thunder on the east.

(The music ceases)

Give me thy hand, dear one, though unto pain
I crush it to be sure that this be dream,
Knowing 't was Death that passed, and oh, how
     near!

## IN TESLA' S LABORATORY

HERE in the dark what ghostly figures press ! —
   No phantom of the Past, or grim or sad ;
   No wailing spirit of woe ; no specter, clad
In white and wandering cloud, whose dumb distress
Is that its crime it never may confess ;
   No shape from the strewn sea ; nor they that add
   The link of Life and Death,—the tearless mad,
That live nor die in dreary nothingness :

But blessèd spirits waiting to be born—
   Thoughts to unlock the fettering chains of Things
      The Better Time ; the Universal Good.
Their smile is like the joyous break of morn ;
   How fair, how near, how wistfully they brood !
   Listen ! that murmur is of angels' wings.

## THE WISTFUL DAYS

WHAT is there wanting in the Spring?
  The air is soft as yesteryear;
  The happy-nested green is here,
And half the world is on the wing.
  The morning beckons, and like balm
  Are westward waters blue and calm.
Yet something 's wanting in the Spring.

What is it wanting in the Spring?
  O April, lover to us all,
  What is so poignant in thy thrall
When children's merry voices ring?
  What haunts us in the cooing dove
  More subtle than the speech of Love,
What nameless lack or loss of Spring?

Let Youth go dally with the Spring,
  Call her the dear, the fair, the young;
  And all her graces ever sung
Let him, once more rehearsing, sing.
  They know, who keep a broken tryst,
  Till something from the Spring be missed
We have not truly known the Spring.

## "LOVE ONCE WAS LIKE AN APRIL DAWN"

LOVE once was like an April dawn:
   Song throbbed within the heart by rote,
And every tint of rose or fawn
   Was greeted by a joyous note.
      How eager was my thought to see
      Into that morning mystery !

Love now is like an August noon,
   No spot is empty of its shine ;
The sun makes silence seem a boon,
   And not a voice so dumb as mine.
      Yet with what words I'd welcome thee—
      Couldst thou return, dear mystery !

## AN IRISH LOVE-SONG

IN the years about twenty
(When kisses are plenty)
ιe love of an Irish lass fell to my fate —
　So winsome and sightly,
　So saucy and sprightly,
ιe priest was a prophet that christened her Kate.

　Soft gray of the dawning,
　Bright blue of the morning,
ιe sweet of her eye there was nothing to mate;
　A nose like a fairy's,
　A cheek like a cherry's,
ιd a smile — well, her smile was like — nothing but Kate.

　To see her was passion,
　To love her, the fashion;
hat wonder my heart was unwilling to wait!
　And, daring to love her,
　I soon did discover
Katharine masking in mischievous Kate.

No Katy unruly,
But Katharine, truly—
Fond, serious, patient, and even sedate;
With a glow in her gladness
That banishes sadness—
Yet stay !   Should I credit the sunshine to *Kate ?*

Love cannot outlive it,
Wealth cannot o'ergive it—
That saucy surrender she made at the gate.
O Time, be but human,
Spare the girl in the woman !
You gave me my Katharine—leave me my Kate !

# "OH, WASTE NO TEARS"

OH, waste no tears on Pain or Fate,
　Nor yet at Sorrow's dire demand;
Think not to drown Regret with weight
　Of weeping, as the sea the strand;
When was Death's victory less elate
　That Grief o'er-sobbed his grasping hand?

Not for the flaws of life shall fall
　The tear most exquisite—ah, no;
But for its fine perfections all:
　For morning's joyous overflow,
For sunset's fleeting festival,
　And what midwinter moons may show;

For wild-rose breath of Keats's line;
　For Titian's rivalry of June;
For Chopin's tender notes that twine
　The sense in one autumnal tune;
For Brunelleschi's dome divine,
　In wonder planned, with worship hewn.

Save them for heroes—not their blood,
  But for the generous vow it sealed ;
For babes, when mothers say, " This bud
  Will be the blossom of the field " ;
For women, when to Vengeance' flood
  They hold for Guilt a stainless shield.

And when two hearts have closer come,
  Through doubts and mysteries and fears,
Till in one look's delirium
  At last the happy truth appears,
When words are weak and music dumb
  Then perfect love shall speak in tears.

# HER SMILE

THE odor is the rose;
　The smile, the woman.
Delights the bud doth sheathe,
Unfolded, all may breathe.
So joys that none could know
Her smiles on all bestow,
　As though a rose were happy to be human!

## SONG FOR THE GUITAR

I GRIEVE to see these tears—
  Long strangers to thine eye—
These jewels that fond years
  For me could never buy.
Weep, weep, and give thy heart relief.
I grieve, but 't is not for thy grief:

  Not for these tears—they were
    Another's ere they fell—
  But those that never stir
    The fountain where they dwell.
I 'd smile, though thou shouldst weep a sea,
Were but a single tear for me !

# URSULA

I SEE her in the festal warmth to-night,
Her rest all grace, her motion all delight.
Endowed with all the woman's arts that please,
In her soft gown she seems a thing of ease,
Whom sorrow may not reach or evil blight.

To-morrow she will toil from floor to floor
To smile upon the unreplying poor,
To stay the tears of widows, and to be
Confessor to men's erring hearts . . . ah me !
She knows not I am beggar at her door.

# A DARK DAY

Gloom of a leaden sky
   Too heavy for hope to move;
Grief in my heart to vie
   With the dark distress above;
Yet happy, happy am I—
   For I sorrow with her I love.

## THE SURPRISED AVOWAL

WHEN one word is spoken,
    When one look you see,
When you take the token,
    Howe'er so slight it be,
The cage's bolt is broken,
    The happy bird is free.

There is no unsaying
    That love-startled word;
It were idle praying
    It no more be heard;
Yet, its law obeying,
    Who shall blame the bird?

What avails the mending
    Where the cage was weak?
What avails the sending
    Far, the bird to seek,
When every cloud is lending
    Wings toward yonder peak?

Thrush, could they recapture
   You to newer wrong,
How could you adapt your
   Strain to suit the throng?
Gone would be the rapture
   Of unimprisoned song.

.

## THE BLOSSOM OF THE SOUL

THOU half-unfolded flower
  With fragrance-laden heart,
What is the secret power
  That doth thy petals part?
What gave thee most thy hue—
The sunshine, or the dew?

Thou wonder-wakened soul!
  As Dawn doth steal on Night
On thee soft Love hath stole.
  Thine eye, that blooms with light,
What makes its charm so new—
Its sunshine, or its dew?

## "I JOURNEYED SOUTH TO MEET THE SPRING"

I JOURNEYED South to meet the Spring,
  To feel the soft tide's gentle rise
That to my heart again should bring,
Foretold by many a whispering wing,
  The old, the new, the sweet surprise.

For once, the wonder was not new—
  And yet it wore a newer grace:
For all its innocence of hue,
Its warmth and bloom and dream and dew,
  I had but left—in Helen's face.

# PARAPHRASES FROM THE SERVIAN

OF

## ZMAI IOVAN IOVANOVICH

AFTER LITERAL TRANSLATIONS

BY

## NIKOLA TESLA

# INTRODUCTORY NOTE

## BY

## Mr. TESLA

# ZMAI IOVAN IOVANOVICH

HARDLY is there a nation which has met with a sadder fate than the Servian. From the height of its splendor, when the empire embraced almost the entire northern part of the Balkan peninsula and a large portion of the territory now belonging to Austria, the Servian nation was plunged into abject slavery, after the fatal battle of 1389 at the Kosovo Polje, against the overwhelming Asiatic hordes. Europe can never repay the great debt it owes to the Servians for checking, by the sacrifice of their own liberty, that barbarian influx. The Poles at Vienna, under Sobieski, finished what the Servians attempted, and were similarly rewarded for their service to civilization.

It was at the Kosovo Polje that Milosh Obilich, the noblest of Servian heroes, fell, after killing the Sultan Murat II. in the very midst of his great army. Were it not that it is an historical fact, one would be apt to consider this episode a myth, evolved by contact with the Greek and Latin races. For in Milosh we see both

43

Leonidas and Mucius, and, more than this, a martyr, for he does not die an easy death on the battle-field like the Greek, but pays for his daring deed with a death of fearful torture.   It is not astonishing that the poetry of a nation capable of producing such heroes should be pervaded with a spirit of nobility and chivalry.   Even the indomitable Marko Kraljevich, the later incarnation of Servian heroism, when vanquishing Musa, the Moslem chief, exclaims, " Woe unto me, for I have killed a better man than myself! "

From that fatal battle until a recent period, it has been black night for the Servians, with but a single star in the firmament—Montenegro.   In this gloom there was no hope for science, commerce, art, or industry. What could they do, this brave people, save to keep up the weary fight against the oppressor?   And this they did unceasingly, though the odds were twenty to one. Yet fighting  merely satisfied their wilder  instincts. There was one more thing they could do, and did : the noble feats of their ancestors, the brave deeds of those who fell in the struggle for liberty, they embodied in immortal song.   Thus circumstances and innate qualities made the Servians a nation of thinkers and poets, and thus, gradually, were evolved their magnificent national poems, which were first collected by their most prolific writer, Vuk Stefanovich Karajich, who also compiled the first dictionary of the Servian tongue, containing more than sixty thousand words.   These national poems Goethe considered fit to match the finest productions of the Greeks and Romans.   What would he have thought of them had he been a Servian?

While the Servians have been distinguished in national

poetry, they have also had many individual poets who attained greatness.   Of contemporaries there is none who has grown so dear to the younger generation as Zmai Iovan Iovanovich.   He was born in Novi Sad (Neusatz), a city at the southern border of Hungary, on November 24, 1833.   He comes from an old and noble family, which is related to the Servian royal house.   In his earliest childhood he showed a great desire to learn by heart the Servian national songs which were recited to him, and even as a child he began to compose poems. His father, who was a highly cultivated and wealthy gentleman, gave him his first education in his native city.   After this he went to Budapest, Prague, and Vienna, and in these cities he finished his studies in law. This was the wish of his father, but his own inclinations prompted him to take up the study of medicine.   He then returned to his native city, where a prominent official position was offered him, which he accepted; but so strong were his poetical instincts that a year later he abandoned the post to devote himself entirely to literary work.

His literary career began in 1849, his first poem being printed in 1852, in a journal called " Srbski Letopis " ("Servian Annual Review"); to this and to other journals, notably " Neven " and "Sedmica," he contributed his early productions.   From that period until 1870, besides his original poems, he made many beautiful translations from Petefy and Arany, the two greatest of the Hungarian poets, and from the Russian of Lermontof, as well as from German and other poets.   In 1861 he edited the comic journal, " Komarac " (" The Mosquito "), and in the same year he started the literary journal, "Javor," and to these papers he contributed many beautiful poems. In 1861 he married, and during the few happy years that followed he produced his admirable series of lyrical poems called "Giulichi," which probably remain his masterpiece. In 1862, greatly to his regret, he discontinued his beloved journal, "Javor"—a sacrifice which was asked of him by the great Servian patriot, Miletich, who was then active on a political journal, in order to insure the success of the latter.

In 1863 he was elected director of an educational institution, called the Tekelianum, at Budapest. He now ardently renewed the study of medicine at the university, and took the degree of doctor of medicine. Meanwhile he did not relax his literary labors. Yet, for his countrymen, more valuable even than his splendid productions were his noble and unselfish efforts to nourish the enthusiasm of Servian youth. During his stay in Budapest he founded the literary society Preodnica, of which he was president, and to which he devoted a large portion of his energies.

In 1864 he started his famous satirical journal, "Zmai" ("The Dragon"), which was so popular that the name became a part of his own. In 1866 his comic play "Sharan" was given with great success. In 1872 he had the great pain of losing his wife, and, shortly after, his only child. How much these misfortunes affected him is plainly perceptible from the deeply sad tone of the poems which immediately followed. In 1873 he started another comic journal, the "Ziza." During the year 1877 he began an illustrated chronicle of the Russo-Turkish war, and in 1878 appeared his popular comic journal, " Starmali." During all this period he wrote not only poems, but much prose, including short novels, often under an assumed name. The best of these is probably " Vidosava Brankovicheva." In recent years he has published a great many charming little poems for children.

Since 1870 Zmai has pursued his profession as a physician. He is an earnest advocate of cremation, and has devoted much time to the furtherance of that cause. Until recently he was a resident of Vienna, but now he is domiciled in Belgrade. There he lives the life of a true poet, loving all and beloved by everybody. In recognition of his merit, the nation has voted him a subvention.

The poems of Zmai are so essentially Servian that to translate them into another tongue appears next to impossible. In keen satire free from Voltairian venom, in good-hearted and spontaneous humor, in delicacy and depth of expression, they are remarkable. Mr. Johnson has undertaken the task of versifying a few of the shorter ones after my literal and inadequate readings. Close translation being often out of the question, he has had to paraphrase, following as nearly as possible the original motives and ideas. In some instances he has expanded in order to complete a picture or to add a touch of his own. The poems which follow will give some idea of the versatility of the Servian poet, but come far short of indicating his range.

*Nikola Tesla.*

NEW YORK CITY.

# THE THREE GIAOURS

In the midst of the dark and stormy night
Feruz Pacha awakes in fright,
And springs from out his curtained bed.
The candle trembles as though it read
Upon his pallid face the theme
And terror of his nightly dream.

He calls to his startled favorite:
"The keys ! the keys of the dungeon-pit !
Cannot those cursèd Giaours stay
There in their own dark, rotting away,
Where I gave them leave three years ago ?
Had I but buried their bones ! —but, no !
They come at midnight to clatter and creep,
And haunt and threaten me in my sleep."

" Pacha, wait till the morning light !
Do not go down that fearful flight

Where every step is a dead man's moan !
Mujo to-morrow will gather each bone
And bury it deep.  Let the Giaours freeze
If thy bed be warm."

                  " Nay, give me the keys.
Girl, you talk like a wrinkled dame
That shudders at whisper of a name.
When they were living, their curses made
A thousand cowards: was I afraid ?
Now they are dead, shall my fear begin
With the Giaour's curse, or the skeleton's grin ?
No, I must see them face to face
In the very midst of their dwelling-place,
And find what need they have of me
That they call my name eternally."

As groping along to the stair he goes,
The light of the shaking candle shows
A face like a white and faded rose ;
But if this be fear, it is fear to stay,
For something urges him on his way—
Though the steps are cold and the echoes mock—
Till the right key screams in the rusted lock.

Ugh ! what a blast from the dungeon dank ! —
From the place where Hunger and Death were wed
Whence even the snakes by instinct fled,

While the very lizards crouched and shrank
In a chill of terror. 'T is inky black
And icy cold, but he cannot go back,
For there, as though the darkness flowers—
There sit the skeletons of three Giaours
Ghost-white in the flickering candle-gleam ! —
(Or is it the remnant of his dream ?)
About a stone that is green with mold
They sit in a group, and their fingers hold
Full glasses, and as the glasses clink
The first Giaour beckons him to drink.

" Pacha, here is a glass for thee !
    When last on me the sunlight shone
I had a wife who was dear to me.
    She was alone—no, not alone ;
The blade in her hand was her comrade true,
As she came to your castle, seeking you.

" And when she came to your castle gate
    She dared you forth, but you would not go.
Fiend and coward, you could not wait
    For a woman's wrath, but shot her, so.
Her heart fell down in a piteous flood.
This glass is filled with her precious blood.

" See how fine as I hold it up !
Drink, Feruz Pacha, the brimming cup !"

Spellbound the Pacha now draws nigh;
He empties the glass with a sudden cry:
The skeletons drink with a laugh and toss,
And they make the sign of the holy cross.

Then speaks the second of the dead:
    " When to this darkness I was led,
        My mother asked, 'What sum will give
    Your prisoner back to the sun ? ' You said,
        'Three measures of gold, and the dog shall
            live.'
    Through pinching toil by noon and night
    She saved and saved till her hope grew bright.

    " But when she brought you the yellow hoard,
        You mocked at the drops on her tired brow,
    And said, 'Toward the pay for his wholesome
            board
    Of good round stones I will this allow.'
    She died while her face with toil was wet.
    This glass is filled with her faithful sweat.

    " See how fine as I hold it up !
    Drink, Feruz Pacha, the brimming cup ! "

Haggard the Pacha now stands by;
He drains the glass with a stifled cry:

Again they drink with a laugh and toss,
And the third one says, as his comrades cross:

"When this black shadow on me fell,
    There sang within my mountain home
My one pale lad.  Bethought him well
    That he would to my rescue come;
But when he tried to lift the gun
He tottered till the tears would run.

"Though vengeance sped his weary feet,
    Too late he came.  Then back he crept,—
Forgot to drink, forgot to eat,—
    And no slow moment went unwept.
He died of grief at his meager years.
This glass is laden with his tears.

"See how fine as I hold it up !
Drink, Feruz Pacha, the brimming cup !"

The Pacha staggers; he holds it high;
He drinks; he falls with a moan and cry:
They laugh, they cross, but they drink no more—
For the dead in the dungeon-cave are four.

# LUKA FILIPOV

(AN INCIDENT OF THE MONTENEGRIN WAR OF 1876–78)

ONE more hero to be part
    Of the Servians' glory !
Lute to lute and heart to heart
    Tell the homely story;
Let the Moslem hide for shame,
Trembling like the falcon's game,
Thinking on the falcon's name—
    Luka Filipov.

When he fought with sword and gun
    Doughty was he reckoned;
When *he* was the foremost, none
    Blushed to be the second.
But he tired of the taint
Of the Turk's blood, learned restraint
From his sated sword—the quaint
    Luka Filipov.

Thus he reasoned : Though they fall
  Like the grass in mowing,
Yet the dead Turks, after all,
  Make a sorry showing.
Foes that die remember not
How our Montenegrins bought
Our unbroken freedom—thought
    Luka Filipov.


So, in last year's battle-storm
  Swooped our Servian falcon,
Chose the sleekest of the swarm
  From beyond the Balkan :
Plucked a pacha from his horse,
Carried him away by force,
While we cheered along his course :
    " Luka !" " Filipov !"


To the Prince his prize he bore
  Just as he had won him—
Laid him at the Prince's door,
  Not a scratch upon him.
" Prince, a present !　And for fear
He should find it lonely here,
I will fetch his mate," said queer
    Luka Filipov.

Back into the fight he rushed
    Where the Turks were flying,
Past his kinsmen boldly brushed,
    Leaping dead and dying:
Seized a stalwart infidel,
Wrenched his gun and, like a spell,
Marched him back—him heeding well
    Luka Filipov.

But the Moslems, catching breath
    Mid their helter-skelter,
Poured upon him hail of death'
    From a rocky shelter,
Till a devil-guided ball
Striking one yet wounded all:
For there staggered, nigh to fall,
    Luka Filipov !

Paused the conflict—all intent
    On the two before us;
And the Turkish regiment
    Cheered in hideous chorus
As the prisoner, half afraid,
Turned and started up the glade,
Thinking—dullard ! —to evade
    Luka Filipov.

We 'd have fired—but Luka's hand
  Rose in protestation,
While his pistol's mute command
  Needed no translation ;
For the Turk retraced his track,
Knelt and took upon his back
(As a peddler shifts his pack)
    Luka Filipov !

How we cheered him as he passed
  Through the line, a-swinging
Gun and pistol—bleeding fast—
  Grim—but loudly singing :
" Lucky me to find a steed
Fit to give the Prince for speed !
Rein or saddle ne'er shall need
    Luka Filipov ! "

So he urged him to the tent
  Where the Prince was resting—
Brought his captive, shamed and spent,
  To make true his jesting.
And as couriers came to say
That our friends had won the day,
Who should up and faint away ?
    Luka Filipov.

# A MOTHER OF BOSNIA

### I

THREE sons she has of Servian mold
　As balsam for her widow's grief,
While in her Danka all behold
　A treasure precious past belief.

Oh, lovely Danka ! happy she,
　More fortunate than all beside,
To be the pride of brothers three,
　Themselves of Bosnia the pride !

In her they glory; she inspires
　To freedom's never-ending fight,
And in their hearts burn patriot fires,
　As stars upon the Turkish night.

And often at the mother's door
　Tears mingle with the words that bless :

" O gods of battle ! guard my four—
My falcons and my falconess."


II


HER radiant beauty nothing hides—
  What wonder that the Turk has seen,
And as before her door he rides
  The Raven-Aga calls her queen !

For three nights has he lain awake—
  To call on Allah ?   Nay, till dawn
Calling on Danka, for whose sake
  His heart is sore, his brow is wan.

He gathers warriors ere the sun ;
  They gallop quickly through the murk ;
And Danka, at the signal-gun,
  Cries, " Save me, brothers ! —'tis the Turk ! "

Now flash the rifles, speeds the fight,
  Till, shamed, the Raven-Aga flies.
Alas for Danka ! in her sight
  One lion-hearted brother dies.
    .    .    .    .    .    .    .

Again the infidel appears,
   And at his heels ride forty guns;
But at the voice of Danka's fears
   Red many a Turkish stirrup runs.

But, oh, at vespers, when once more
   The baffled Raven back has fled,
Across the sill of Danka's door
   There lies another brother, dead.

.     .     .     .     .     .     .

The Turkish devil once again
   Summons each savage wedding-guest,
And half a hundred to be slain
   Go forth at midnight toward the west.

Once more the stealthy Moslems ride,
   Once more the Servians gather fast,
As Danka summons to her side
   Her brother—and her last.

The fight grows fiercer, till the dead
   Fill the dim street from wall to wall.
Call on thy mother, Battle-wed—
   Thou hast no brother left to call !

The Raven seizes her and croaks:
   " At last thou art my bride, proud maid !"

" Not thine—my yataghan's ! "  Two strokes—
Her warm heart weds the loyal blade.

### III

DARK is the night as on the slopes
  Of that deserted battle-ground
The mother, crazed with sorrow, gropes
  Until her sons' three swords are found.

And as she roams through Servian lands
  (Her mirth more piteous than tears)
She bears a blade in her thin hands
  To right the wrongs of many years.

And offering Danka's plighted knife
  Or one of those three patriot swords,
She calls the coldest rock to strife,—
  " Take, and repel the Turkish hordes ! "

And as the rock no word replies,
  She asks, " Are you not Servian too ?
Why are you silent then ? " she cries;
  " Is there no living heart in you ? "

She treads the dreary night alone ;
There is no echo to her moan. . . .
Is every heart a heart of stone ?

## THE MONSTER

" IN place of the heart, a serpent;
  Rage—for the mind's command;
An eye aflame with wildness;
  A weapon in the hand;

" A brow with midnight clouded;
  On the lips a cynic smile
That tells of a curse unmatchable—
  Born of a sin most vile.

" Of longing, or hope, or virtue,
  No vestige may there be;
You, even in vice inhuman—
  What can you want of me ?

" You in its maddest moment
  The Deepest Pit designed,—
Let loose to sow confusion
  In the order of mankind;

" Here Hatred found you crawling
   Like vermin, groveling, prone,
Filled you with blood of others
   And poisoned all your own.

" Your very thoughts are fiendish—
   Smoke of the fires of Hell.
Weird as you are, how is it
   I seem to know you well ?

" Why with your wild delirium
   Do you infect my sleep ?
Why with my daily footstep
   An equal measure keep ? "

.    .    .    .    .

The monster mutely beckons me
   Back with his ghostly hand,
And dreading his fearful answer
   I heed the grim command.

" Nay, softly," he says; " I pray thee,
   Silence thy frightened moan,
And wipe the sweat from thy forehead ;
   My kinsman thou, my own!

" Look at me well, good cousin ;
    Such wert thou fashioned of ! '
Thou, too, wouldst me resemble
    Without that magic—Love!"

## TWO DREAMS

DEEP on the bosom of Jeel-Begzad
  (Darling daughter of stern Bidar)
Sleeps the rose of her lover lad.
  It brings this word : When the zenith-star
Melts in the full moon's rising light,
Then shall her Giaour come—to-night.

What is the odor that fills her room ?
  Ah ! 't is the dream of the sleeping rose :
To feel his lips near its velvet bloom
  In the secret shadow no moonbeam knows,
Till the maiden passion within her breast
Kindles to flame where the kisses rest.

By the stealthy fingers of old Bidar
  (Savage father of Jeel-Begzad)—
Never bloodless in peace or war—
  Was a handjar sheathed ; and each one had
Graved on its handle a Koran prayer—
He can feel it now, in his ambush there !

The moon rides pale in the quiet night;
   It puts out the stars, but never the gleam
Of the waiting blade's foreboding light,
   Astir in its sheath in a horrid dream
Of pain, of blood, and of gasping breath,
Of the thirst of vengeance drenched in death.

   .    .    .    .    .    .    .    .

The dawn did the dream of the rose undo,
But the dream of the sleeping blade came true.

## MYSTERIOUS LOVE

INTO the air I breathed a sigh;
  She, afar, another breathed—
Sighs that, like a butterfly,
Each went wandering low and high,
  Till the air with sighs was wreathed.

When each other long they sought,
  On a star-o'er-twinkled hill
Jasmine, trembling with the thought,
Both within her chalice caught,
  A lover's potion to distil.

Drank of this a nightingale,
  Guided by the starlight wan—
Drank and sang from dale to dale,
Till every streamlet did exhale
  Incense to the waking dawn.

Like the dawn, the maiden heard;
  While, afar, I felt the fire

In the bosom of the bird;
Forth our sighs again were stirred
  With a sevenfold desire.

These we followed till we learned
  Where they trysted; there erelong
Their fond nightingale returned.
Deeper then our longings burned,
  Deeper the delights of song.

Now, when at the wakening hour,
  Sigh to sigh, we greet his lay,
Well we know its mystic power—
Feeling dawn and bird and flower
  Pouring meaning into May.

Jasmine, perfume every grove !
  Nightingale, forever sing ·
To the brightening dawn above
Of the mystery of love
  In the mystery of spring !

# THE COMING OF SONG

WHEN the sky darkened on the first great sin,
And gates that shut man out shut Hope within,
Like to the falcon when his wing is broke,
The bitter cry of mortals then awoke:
"Too heavy is our burden," groaned the two.
"Shall woes forever on our track pursue,
And nest within these empty hearts?   Or, worse,
Shall we be withered by the cruel curse?
Already less than human, shall we fall
By slow succession to some animal?"

Then, filled with pity at the desperate cry,
Came from His throne of thunder the Most High:
"That you should suffer" (spake the Voice) "is just:
'T is you have chosen for a feast a crust.
But not so unrelenting I—the least
Of all your kind shall be above the beast.
That erring mortals be not lost in fear,
Come from My shining courts, O daughter dear!

Thou dost to heaven, shalt to earth belong."
She came; she stayed: it was the Muse of Song.

Again the day was radiant with light,
And something more than stars illumed the night.
Hope, beckoning, to the desert took its flight.

Where is Pain and dire Distress,
Song shall soothe like soft caress;
Though the stoutest courage fails,
Song 's an anchor in all gales;
When all others fail to reach,
Song shall be the thrilling speech;
Love and friends and comfort fled,
Song shall linger by your bed;
And when Doubt shall question, Why?
Song shall lift you to the sky.

## CURSES

FAIN would I curse thee, sweet unkind!
  That thou art fair;
Fain curse my mother, that not blind
  She did me bear;
But, no ! —each curse would break, not bind,
  The heart ye share.

## A FAIRY FROM THE SUN-SHOWER

[When the Servians see the sun-rays of a summer shower they say it is the fairies combing their hair.]

OVER the meadow a shower is roaming;
    Just beyond is the summer sun;
Fair is the hair that the fays are combing—
    Myth come true ! here 's my dainty one
Tripping the path in the wind's soft blowing;
Her slender form through her gown is showing,
Her foot scarce whispers the way she 's going.
    " Come, my bright one, come, my soul,
    Let my kisses be your goal."

But the path has heard my sighing,
    Turns aside, and leads my fay
Into the forest, love defying.
    Path, accursèd be ! — but stay !
Lost to love each moment gliding,
What if in the woodland hiding
Still for me my fay be biding ! . . .
    " Wait, my bright one, wait, my soul,
    Your sweet kisses are my goal."

## "WHY," YOU ASK, "HAS NOT THE SERVIAN PERISHED ?"

FRAGMENT FROM THE "GIULICHE" ("JEWELS")

"WHY," you ask, "has not the Servian perished,
  Such calamities about him throng ? "
With the sword alike the lyre he cherished :
  He is saved by Song!

## "I BEGGED A KISS OF A LITTLE MAID"

I BEGGED a kiss of a little maid;
   Shyly, sweetly, she consented;
Then of a sudden, all afraid,
   After she gave it, she repented;
And now as penance for that one kiss
She asks a poem—I 'll give her this.

But how can my song be my very best
   When she, with a voice as soft as Circe's,
Has charmed the heart from my lonely breast—
   The heart, the fountain of all true verses ?
Why, oh, why should a maid do this ?
No—I must give her back her kiss.

## WHY THE ARMY BECAME QUIET

SOME said they did but play at war,—
　How that may be, ah ! who can tell ?
I know the gallant army corps
　Upon their fleeing foemen fell,
And sacked their camp, and took their town,
And won both victory and renown.

Now home returning, wild with song,
　They come, the colors flying free.
But as within the door they throng,
　Why does the army suddenly
Hush the fierce din, and silence keep ?—
Why, little brother is asleep.

## THE GIPSY PRAISES HIS HORSE

You 're admiring my horse, sir, I see.
    He 's so light that you 'd think it 's a bird—
Say a swallow.   Ah me !
    He 's a prize !
    It 's absurd
To suppose you can take him all in as he passes
    With the best pair of eyes,
    Or the powerful aid
Of your best pair of glasses :
    Take 'em off, and let 's trade.


What !   " Is Selim as good as he seems ? "
    Never fear,
    Uncle dear,
He 's as good as the best of your dreams,
    And as sound as your sleep.
    It 's only that kind that a gipsy would keep.
The emperor's stables can't furnish his mate.
But his grit and his gait,

And his wind and his ways,
A gipsy like me does n't know how to praise.
But (if truth must be told)
Although you should cover him over with gold
He 'd be worth one more sovereign still.

                        " Is he old ? "

Oh, don't look at his teeth, my dear sir !
   I never have seen 'em myself.
   Age has nothing to do with an elf;
      So it 's fair to infer
My fairy can never grow old.
Oh, don't look—(Here, my friend,
Will you do me the kindness to hold
For a moment these reins while I 'tend
   To that fly on his shanks ?) . . .
   As I said—(Ah—now—thanks !)
     The longer you drive
     The better he 'll thrive.
He 'll never be laid on the shelf !
   The older that colt is, the younger he 'll grow.
   I 've tried him for years, and I know.

" Eat ? Eat ? " do you say ?
Oh, that nag is n't nice
About eating !  Whatever you have will suffice.

He takes everything raw—
Some oats or some hay,
    Or a small wisp of straw,
    If you have it.   If not, never mind—
Selim won't even neigh.
What kind of a feeder is he ?   That 's the kind !

" Is he clever at jumping a fence ? "
What a question to ask !   He 's immense
    At a leap !
    How absurd !
    Why, the trouble 's to keep
Such a Pegasus down to the ground.
He takes every fence at a bound
      With the grace of a bird ;
    And so great is his strength,
    And so keen is his sense,
    He goes over a fence
Not across, but the way of its length !

" Under saddle ? "   No saddle for Selim !
Why, you 've only to mount him, and feel him
    Fly level and steady, to see
    What disgrace that would be.
No, you could n't more deeply insult him, unless
You attempted to guess
    And pry into his pedigree.

Now why should you speak of his eyes ?
    Does he seem like a horse that would need
    An eye-glass to add to his speed
Or, perchance, to look wise ?
    No indeed.
    Why, not only 's the night to that steed
Just the same as the day,
    But he knows all that passes—
Both before and behind, either way.
    Oh, he does n't need glasses !

" Has he any defect ? "   What a question, my friend !
    That is why, my dear sir, I am willing to sell.
    You know very well
It is only the horse that you give or you lend
That has glanders, or springhalt, or something to mend :
    'T is because not a breath
    Of defect or of death
Can be found on my Selim that he 's at your pleasure.
Alas ! not for gipsies the care of such treasure.

And now about speed.   " Is he fast ? "   I should say !
Just listen—I 'll tell you.
                         One equinox day,
Coming home from Erdout in the usual way,
A terrible storm overtook us.  'T was plain
There was nothing to do but to run for it.  Rain,

Like the blackness of night, gave us chase.   But that nag,
Though he 'd had a hard day, did n't tremble or sag.
    Then the lightning would flash,
    And the thunder would crash
    With a terrible din.
They were eager to catch him ; but he would just neigh,
Squint back to make sure, and then gallop away.
Well, this made the storm the more furious yet,
And we raced and we raced, but he was n't upset,
    And he would n't give in !
At last when we got to the foot of the hill
    At the end of the trail,
By the stream where our white gipsy castle was set,
And the boys from the camp came a-waving their caps,
    At a word he stood still,
To be hugged by the girls and be praised by the chaps.
    We had beaten the gale,
And Selim was dry as a bone—well, perhaps,
    Just a little bit damp on the tip of his tail.*

  * Readers will be reminded by this conclusion of Mark Twain's
story of the fast horse as told to him by Oudinot, of the Sandwich
Islands, and recorded in " The Galaxy " for April, 1871.   In that
veracious narrative it is related that not a single drop fell on the
driver, but the dog was swimming behind the wagon all the way.

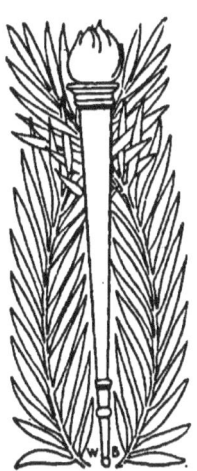

# THE VOICE OF WEBSTER

## THE VOICE OF WEBSTER

SILENCE was envious of the only voice
That mightier seemed than she.   So, cloaked as Death,
With potion borrowed from Oblivion,
Yet with slow step and tear-averted look,
She sealed his lips, closed his extinguished eyes,
And veiling him with darkness, deemed him dead.
But no! — There 's something vital in the great
That blunts the edge of Death, and sages say
You should stab deep if you would kill a king.
In vain!   The conqueror's conqueror he remains,
Surviving his survivors.   And as when,
The prophet gone, his least disciple stands
Newly invested with a twilight awe,
So linger men beside his listeners
While they recount that miracle of speech
And the hushed wonder over which it fell.

What do they tell us of that mighty voice?
Breathing an upper air, wherein he dwelt
'Mid shifting clouds a mountain of resolve,
And falling like Sierra's April flood

That pours in ponderous cadence from the cliff,
Waking Yosemite from its sleep of snow,
And less by warmth than by its massive power
Thawing a thousand torrents into one.
Such was his speech, and were his fame to die
Such for its requiem alone were fit:
Some kindred voice of Nature, as the Sea
When autumn tides redouble their lament
On Marshfield shore; some elemental force
Kindred to Nature in the mind of man—
A far-felt, rhythmic, and resounding wave
Of Homer, or a freedom-breathing wind
Sweeping the height of Milton's loftiest mood.
Most fit of all, could his own words pronounce
His eulogy, eclipsing old with new,
As though a dying star should burst in light.

And yet he spoke not only with his voice.
His full brow, buttressing a dome of thought,
Moved the imagination like the rise
Of some vast temple covering nothing mean.
His eyes were sibyls' caves, wherein the wise
Read sibyls' secrets; and the iron clasp
Of those broad lips, serene or saturnine,
Made proclamation of majestic will.
His glance could silence like a frowning Fate.

His mighty frame was refuge, while his mien
Did make dispute of stature with the gods.

See, in the Senate, how his presence towers
Above the tallest, who but seem as marks :
To guide the unwonted gaze to where he stands,
First of his peers—a lordly company.
Each State still gave the others of its best—
Our second race of giants, now, alas!
Buried beneath the lava-beds of war.
Not yet had weaklings trod the purchased path
To a feigned honor in the curule chair,
Holding a world's contempt of them for fame —
As one should take the leaves stripped from his scourge
To wreathe himself a counterfeit of bay.
An age is merely Man, and, thus compact,
Must grimly expiate paternal sins ;
That age's shame stands naked to the world,
And no man dares to hide it ; yet one boast
Palsies the pointing finger of to-day :
*'T was slave, not master, that we bought and sold.*

Oh for fit word of scorn to execrate
Our brood new-born of Greed and Liberty!
Not the blind mass of stumbling ignorance
(For the dread portent of a blackening cloud

May by bold shafts of sunlight be dispersed),
But those who lead them to the nation's hurt—
These our kind neighbors, semblances of men,
The Church's bulwark, the beloved of homes,
Locked fast in friendship's ever-loyal pledge,
Yet to whom treason is their daily breath.
Not Lucifer, on each conspiring wind
Rallying his abject crew to new assaults;
Not all the recreant names that spawning War
Has cursed with immortality, can match
The craft of their betrayals.   All is sold:
Law, justice, mercy, and the future's hope—
This land that buoys the fainting fears of Man.
Yet to praise Webster one of these has dared!—
Webster, undaunted by the hour's reproof,
Webster, untempted by the hour's applause,
Who scorned to win by any art but truth!
Who, had he heard the impious flattery,
Across the Senate would have launched his wrath,
Like Cicero on cowering Catiline,
In one white passion that forevermore
Had saved to Infamy an empty name
That now he spurns in silence from his grave.

Yet had he frailties, which let those recount
Who have not seen the nigh-o'erwhelmèd state

Rescued from peril by some roisterer's skill
While all the petted virtues of the home
Stood pale and helpless.   Time 's a mountain-wall
That gives a fainter echo to one's best,
But to what 's weak or wanting, mere disdain.
He had his passions—all but one are dead:
That was his country.   Never lover loved,
Soldier defended, poet praised, as he,
Who marveled all should worship not his queen,
And much forgave to any loving her.
And when, one desperate day, the threatening hand
His hand so long arrested, he being gone,
Felt 'neath its pillow for the unsheath'd sword,
Who spoke for Union but with Webster's voice?
Who struck for Union but with Webster's arm?
Forgetful of the father in the son,
Men praised in Lincoln what they blamed in him.
And though, his natural tenderness grown grave,
He lives not in Love's immortality
Like Lincoln, shrined within his foeman's heart;
Though he trod not the path of him whose soul
Triumphed in song that beckoned armies on
More than persuading drum, dare-devil fife,
Or clarion bugle; though no battle-flame
Rose to a peak in him: yet was his blood
In heroes and his wrath in righteous war.

Then did the vision of his patriot hope,
Pictured in pleading but in warning words,
Inspire the inspirers, nerve the halting brave,
Make triflers solemn with the choice of death.
And when at last came Peace, the friend of all,
Grateful and wondrous as first drops of rain
After the long starvation of the drought,
Men harkened back to that prophetic hour
When two protagonists, like chosen knights,
Made long and suave epitome of war:
When Hayne arose 't was Sumter's gun was heard,
When Webster closed 't was Appomattox field.

But oh, his larger triumph was to come!
His voice, in victory potent, was in peace
Predominant.   His all-benignant thought
That, never wavering through the strife of words,
No Alleghanies, no Potomac knew,
Searching the future to bring olive back,
Lived like a fragrance in the heart of Grant,
And at the perilous moment of success.
Pointed the path to concord from the grave.
And what famed concord! —not a grudging truce,
Nor interlude of hate, but peace divine:
When hands still wet with blood again were clasped,
Each foe forgiving what is ne'er forgot;

The hacked sword eager for the scabbard's rest,
Not from the fear, but for the love of man.
A loftier conquest of the Blue that warred
For freedom, not for conquest!  Victory,
Unsought, of all the hardly vanquished Gray!
Marvel of Europe staggering in arms;
Message of Hope unto the souls that herd
Dumb at the slaughter for the whim of kings;
Lusus of History until wars shall cease.
My country! since nor memory of strife,
Nor natural vengeance, nor the orphan's tears
Can from Love's nobler triumph hale thee back:
Who worthier than thou to lead the way
Unto the everlasting Truce of God,
When brothers shall toward brothers over sea
Stretch not the sword-blade, but the open palm,
Till on Time's long but ever-upward slope
They mount together to unreckoned heights,
And grateful nations gladly follow them !

.     .     .     .     .     .     .     .

Thus sang I, proud to be but one of all
The sands upon a shore whereon there breaks,
Freighted with purpose vast, the will of Heaven—
When a rude clash I heard, that yet I hear,
When Discord grasped again her rusted harp
And struck new terror from the raveled strings,

Calling Ambition blindfold to the lead
Of Want, Dishonor, Perfidy, and Crime,
Who in their turn misguide the innocent,
Groping their way by the last firebrands
Plucked from their holocaust of hoarded truth.
The air we thought as peaceful as the noon
Was dark with sudden hatred, as with cloud
Blown, in long-gathered tempest, from the West,
Like a wild storm of summer heat and wind
Circling in passion, bruited by dismay,
And dragging death and chaos in its train,
As some old myth of savagery come true,
And Nature had turned demon, rending Man.

This madness Webster still can medicine,
Who was physician to its earlier taint.
He did not fury then with fury meet,
But to the sanity of eternal law
Wooed back the wandering mind.   Who could forget
His calming presence when, ere he began,
Confusion fled before his morning look
Of power miraculously new and mild;
The speech as temperate as a wind of May;
The mind as candid as the noonday light;
The tones deliberate, confident, sedate,
Waking no passion, and yet moving all

'ith such a high compulsion that at last
eason, the king that well-nigh had been lost
'pon the confines of his sovereign realm,
emounted to the throne with steady step,
nd men again were proud of his control.

), in these days of hopeful hearts' despair,
'hen perils threat, ay, throng the ship of state,
nd less from gale without than torch within,
'ho—who but Webster with his faith serene
iall rouse the sleeping to command their fate,
iall bid them steer by the unswerving stars,
nd in them troth with Liberty renew?
iagination gave his spirit wings,
iat, seeing past the tempest and the flame,
e might remind us of our destiny:
) save from faction what was meant for Man;
) cherish brotherhood simplicity,
ie chance for each that is the hope for all;
) guard the realm from Sloth, and Greed, and Waste—
iose sateless Gorgons of democracy;
nd above all, whatever storm may rage,
) cling to Law, the path of Liberty,
ie prop of heaven, the very pulse of God.
ius our new soil, the home of every seed,
here first the whole world meets on equal terms,

Shall such new marvels show of man's estate
In knowledge, wisdom, beauty, virtue, power,
The Past shall fade in pity or in scorn,
While fresher joys shall thrill the pulse of earth.

No, Webster's fame not Webster's self can blot.
Fair is perfection's image in the soul,
And yearning for it holds the world to good.
Yet is it such a jewel as may not
Unto a single guardian be entrust,
But to the courage of a multitude
Who all together have what each may lack.
Though men may falter, it is Virtue's strength
To be indelible: our smallest good
By our worst evil cannot be undone.
The discords of that life—how short they fall,
Like ill-strung arrows!    But its harmonies—
Harmonious speech large with harmonious thought—
Dwell in a nation's peace, a nation's hope,
Imperishable music; not the rhythm
Of some remembering moment, but the peal
And crash of conflict unforgettable
Piercing the mid and thick of night.    No, no,
That voice of thunder died not with the storm,
But in the dull and coward times of peace
Long shall its echoes rouse the patriot's heart.

# HANDS ACROSS SEA

.

The War of Independence was virtually a second English civil war. The ruin of the American cause would have been also the ruin of the constitutional cause in England; and a patriotic Englishman may revere the memory of Patrick Henry and George Washington not less justly than the patriotic American.

—JOHN MORLEY, on Burke.

## HANDS ACROSS SEA

### I

ƎNGLAND, thou breeder of heroes and of bards,
Ḣad ever nation manlier shield or song!
'or thee such rivalry have sword and pen,
'ame, from her heaped green, crowns with equal hand
'he deathless deed and the immortal word.
'or which dost thou thy Sidney hold more dear,
)efense of England or of Poesie?
'romwell or Milton—if man's guiding stars
'ould vanish as they came—which wouldst thou spare?
,ost Kempenfelt indeed, were Cowper mute!
'o victory, not alone on shuddering seas
Ṙode Nelson, but on Campbell's tossing rhyme.
Ḣark to thy great Duke's greater dirge, and doubt
'or which was Waterloo the worthier won,
'o change the tyrant on a foreign throne,
)r add a faultless ode to English song.
;reat deeds make poets: by whose nobler word,
n turn, the blood of heroes is transfused

Into the veins of sluggards, till they rise,
Surprised, exalted to the height of men.

Nor can Columbia choose between the two
Which give more glory to thy Minster gloom.
They are our brave, our deathless, our divine—
Our Saxon grasp on their embattled swords,
Our Saxon numbers in their lyric speech.
We grudge no storied wreath, nay, would withhold
Of bay or laurel not one envied leaf.
Then, on thy proud cliff fronting Europe-ward,
Strong in thyself, not by some weaker prop,
Give to the greeting of a kindred voice
A moment in the ebb of thy disdain.

## II

Is it but chance that in thy treasured verse
There is no pæan, no exulting line,
No phrase of martial fervor, to record
The Briton's prowess on our Western shore?
There was no lapse of valiance in thy race—
Or else had Time forgot to mark the years.
Nor hast thou since had lack of many a voice
Whose words, like wings to seed, on every air
From land to hospitable land import

Thy progeny of courage, justice, truth.
Why, then, when all our songs were resonant,
Were all thy singers silent?　Candor, speak!
There is a dæmon makes the Muses dumb
When they would praise the wrong: but Liberty
From Nature has inheritance of speech—
The forest harp, the flood's processional,
The glorious antiphone of every shore.
When these are dumb, then poets may be mute!


### III

TAUGHT by thy heroes, summoned by thy bards,
Against the imperious folly of thy kings
Twice our reluctant banners were arrayed.
What matter if the victors were not thine,
If thine the victories?　Thou art more secure
Saved from the canker of successful wrong.
Thou dost not blush for Naseby, where, of old,
England most conquered, conquering Englishmen.
So when thou hear'st the trumpets in our verse
In praise of our new land's deliverance,
Hard won from Winter, Hunger, and from thee,
And from those allies thou didst hire and scorn,
Deem it not hatred, nor the vulgar pride
Of the arena, nor the greed of fame.

('Twixt men or nations, there 's no victory
Save when an angel overcomes in both.)
Would all our strife were blameless!   Some, alas!
Hath trophies hoarded only to be hid,
For courage cannot hallow wanton war.
Be proud our hand against thee ne'er was raised
But to wrench English justice from thy grasp.
And, as to landsmen, far from windy shores,
The breathing shell may bear the murmuring sea,
Still in our patriot song reverberates
The mighty voice that sang at Hampden's side.


IV

TRUE, there are those of our impassioned blood
Who can forget but slowly that thy great
Misread the omens of our later strife,
And knew not Freedom when she called to thee.
These think they hate thee! — these, who have embraced
Before the altar their fraternal foes!  ·
Not white of York and red of Lancaster
More kindly mingle in thy rose of peace
Than blend in cloudless dawn our blue and gray.
Already Time and History contend
For sinking rampart and the grassy ridge
That with its challenge startles pilgrim feet

Along the fringes of the wounded wood.
The bedtime wonder of our children holds
Vicksburg coeval with the siege of Troy,
And the scorned slave so hastened to forgive
The scar has lost remembrance of the lash.
Since Love has drawn the sting of that distress,
For one with wrath to compass sea and years
Were but to make of injury a jest,
Holding the occasion guiltier than the cause.
But Hate 's a weed that withers in the sun ;
A cell of which the prisoner holds the key,
His will his jailer ; nay, a frowning tower
Invincible by legions, but with still
One secret weakness: *who can hate may love.*
Oh, pausing in thy cordon of the globe,
Let one full drop of English blood be spilled
For Liberty, not England : men would lose
Their fancied hatred in an ardor new,
As Minas Channel turns to Fundy's tide.
Hate thee? Hast thou forgot red Pei-ho's stream,
The triple horror of the ambuscade,
The hell of battle, the foredoomed assault,
When thou didst stand the champion of the world,
Though the awed sea for once deserted thee?
Who then sprang to thee, breaking from the bonds
Of old observance, with a human cry,

Thirsting to share thy glorious defeat
As men are wont to covet victory?
Hate thee?    Hast thou forgot Samoa's reef,
The day more dark than any starless night,
The black storm buffeting the hopeless ships,
The struggle of thy sons, and, as they won,
Gaining the refuge of the furious deep,
The immortal cheers that shook the *Trenton's* deck,
As Death might plead with Nature for the brave?
Stands there no monument upon that strand?
Then let remembrance build a beacon high,
That long its warning message may remind
How common danger stirs the brother heart.


### v


WHY turn the leaf back to an earlier page?
To-day, not moved by memory-or fear,
But by the vision of a nobler time,
Millions cry toward thee in a passion of peace.
We need thee, England, not in armed array
To stand beside us in the empty quarrels
That kings pursue, ere War itself expire
Like an o'er-armored knight in desperate lunge
Beneath the weight of helmet and of lance;
But now, in conflict with an inner foe
Who shall in conquering either conquer both.

For it is written in the book of fate:
*By no sword save her own falls Liberty.*
A wondrous century trembles at its dawn,
Conflicting currents telling its approach;
And while men take new reckonings from the peaks,
Reweigh the jewel and retaste the wine,
Be ours to guard against the impious hands
That, like rash children, tamper with that blade.
Thou, too, hast seen the vision: shall it be
Only a dream, caught in the web of night,
Lost through the coarser meshes of the day?
Or like the beauty of the prismic bow,
Which the sun's ardor, that creates, consumes?
Oh, may it be the thing we image it! —
The beckoning spirit of our common race
Floating before us in a fringe of light
With Duty's brow, Love's eyes, the smile of Peace;
Benignant figure of compelling mien,
Star-crowned, star-girdled, and o'erstrewn with stars,
As though a constellation should descend
To be fit courier to a glorious age.


VI


O THOU that keepest record of the brave,
Something of us to thee is lost, more worth
Than all the fabled wealth of sibyls' leaves.

Not with dull figures, but with heroes' deeds,
Fill up those empty annals.   Teach thy youth
To know not North's but Byron's Washington;
To follow Hale's proud step as tearfully
As we pale André's.   And when next thy sons
Stand in Manhattan gazing at the swirl
Of eddying trade from Trinity's brown porch,
Astonished, with the praise that half defames,
At the material greatness of the scene,—
The roar, the fret, the Babel-towers of trade,—
Let one stretch forth a hand and touch the stone
That covers Lawrence, saying, "To this height
Our English blood has risen."   And to know
The sea still speaks of courage, let them learn
What murmurs it of Craven in one bay,
And what of Cushing shouts another shore.
(Find but one star, how soon the sky is full!
One hero summons hundreds to the field:
So to the memory.)   Let them muse on Shaw,
Whose bones the deep did so begrudge the land
It sent its boldest waves to bring them back
Unto the blue domed Pantheon where they lie,
The while his soul still leads in martial bronze;
Tell them of sweet-dirged Winthrop, whom to name
Is to be braver, as one grows more pure
Breathing the thought of lover or of saint;

Grim Jackson, Covenanter of the South,
And her well-christened Sidney, fallen soon ;
Kearny and Lyon.   Of such hearts as these
Who would not boast were braggart of all else.
Each fought for Right—and conquered with the Best.
Such graves are all the ruins that we have—
Our broken arch and battlement—to tell
That ours, like thine, have come of Arthur's race.

O England, wakened from thy lull of song,
Thy scepter, sword, and spindle, fasces-like,
Bound with fresh laurel as thy sign of strength,
When shalt thou win us with a theme of ours,
Reclaiming thus thine own, till men shall say :
" That was the noblest conquest of her rule " ?

www.ingramcontent.com/pod-product-compliance
Lightning Source LLC
Chambersburg PA
CBHW020803020726
47495CB00008B/2562